Hated
The Surrender Club Series
by
Reba Bale

CW01081714

Copyright

About This Book

They were mortal enemies in high school, but when fate brings them back together years later, passion flares.

Billionaire Zelda Eldrich loves to play with the new submissives at Club Surrender, an exclusive women only BDSM club. She has a reputation as a tough but caring domme who never gets personally involved with her subs. Until Mariah comes in for "newbies night".

Mariah Collins has been dreaming about experiencing her first spanking for years. She's thrilled to score an invitation to visit the "light BDSM" club, but she never expected to run into the woman who she'd tortured all through high school. Back then the bisexual had been confused about her attraction to Zelda, but there's no confusion now. She wants to make a life with the sexy dominatrix...if only Zelda would talk to her.

Punishment turns to love, but when a misunderstanding threatens to turn the two women back into enemies, Zelda's going to need to pull out all the stops to show Mariah that she wants forever.

Hated is book two in the *Surrender Club* instalove lesbian romance series. Each book is a fun and steamy standalone with matchmaking dommes, loving relationships, and a sweet happily ever after.

These books are intended for mature audiences.

Be sure to check out a free preview of Reba Bale's lesbian romance "The Divorcee's First Time" at the end of this book!

Dedication

This book is dedicated to everyone who had a Mariah in high school. Being bullied sucks, but you made it through. And if you ever run into your bully again, remember that spanking is always an option. ☺

Join My Newsletter

Want a free book? Join my weekly newsletter and you'll receive a fun subscriber gift. I promise I will only email you when there are new releases, free books, or special sales you'll want to see.

Visit my newsletter sign-up page at bit.ly/RebaBaleSapphic[1] to join today.

Mariah

"I don't know about this, Amy."

I tugged on my short leather skirt, feeling ridiculous wearing something so sexy when I was practically a middle-aged woman.

"You've been talking about trying out a BDSM club ever since we first read that 50 Shades book. Don't be a chickenshit."

That was my best friend, the epitome of tough love.

Amy and I had first met in college when we were matched as roommates in the dorm and had been inseparable ever since. We'd been through a lot of ups and downs over the last seventeen years, but one thing had been constant: our friendship.

I glanced at my best friend, taking in her long blonde hair that somehow always looked effortlessly good, her trim waist and round breasts that were somehow resisting the ravages of time. Not for the first time, I wished that we were attracted to each other. We were both bisexual and, having lived together for years, we knew we were compatible.

But sadly, there was no heat there. We'd tried kissing each other once in college, right after we'd both had bad break-ups during the same week, but it had been like kissing my sister. Not that I'd ever kissed my sister, just to be clear, but if I had, I was pretty sure there would have been that weird 'ick' factor that I'd felt kissing my best friend.

"Welcome to Club Surrender. Your names please?"

I glanced up at the woman guarding the door. She was built like a linebacker, but her eyes were kind. Club Surrender was one of the premiere BDSM clubs in the country. Two things made it unique. First, it only catered to women, all the clients and even the staff was all women. Second, the club specialized in something they called 'BDSM light'. According to their website, that meant things like spanking, bondage, and flogging but not any of the super hardcore activities that you might find at other clubs.

The founder, a woman named Angela Lewis, had written on the business' website that she wanted to create a club that would be less intimidating for women and avoid the testosterone heavy environments that some other clubs had. I thought it was a genius idea.

Even though all the clubs had rules about communication and consent, I could see where women who'd experienced trauma at the hands of men would be uncomfortable around male dominants. And let's face it, most women had either had a bad experience or knew someone who had.

Amy and I had been trying to get an invite to "Newbies Night" ever since we'd heard about the club from a woman in our book club. I'd lived in Seattle my whole life and had no idea that this was here.

After verifying our identity to the bouncer and signing a consent form we were admitted into the club. I looked around curiously. The placed was jam packed with women of all shapes, sizes, and ages.

The main room was large, with a bar on one side – serving mostly non-alcoholic drinks I knew, since the club strictly prohibited having more than one drink before doing a scene. They had an impressive selection of "mocktails" though.

In the center was a dance floor, crowded with women in various states of dress. To the left there were rows of cushioned seats where at least two people were receiving an over-the-knee spanking and one woman was getting eaten out while a different woman sat on her face. My eyes nearly popped out of my head seeing such uninhibited activity.

The far side of the room was taken up with spanking benches and a couple of structures that I knew were St. Andrew's crosses.

I shivered as I watched someone being flogged at one of the crosses. The flogger, held by a tall dominatrix with long, curly brown hair, moved in a steady rhythm, just hard enough to redden the sub's back but not actually hurt her or break the skin. Her movements were controlled, but somehow the domme radiated power. Meanwhile the submissive, who was completely naked, had a look of ecstasy on her face.

My panties immediately grew damp, and before I could help myself, I moved closer. Something about the domme was calling me over, and I was desperate to get a better look at her.

The woman was wearing a black lace dress, short and tight, with most of her skin visible beneath the peekaboo fabric. She was tall and slim, with a muscular ass and shapely legs. She paused to check on her submissive, speaking low in the woman's ear before nodding and untying the woman's hands from the cross.

The domme turned around and I had an impression of large brown eyes, smooth skin, and a defined jaw with a little dimple right at the point of her chin. And then I gasped.

The dominatrix was my high school crush, Zelda. The girl I'd tortured for years.

Zelda

I could feel someone watching me but kept my focus on my flogger. It wouldn't do to hurt the woman I was scening with on her first night at the club. Well, hurt her more than she wanted. For a first timer, she'd really taken to the flogger. Of course, I'd gone super easy on her, just in case.

Figuring that she'd had enough, I moved close and unbuckled her wrists from the handcuffs that I'd used to restrain her. They were really just nylon straps with buckles, but worked quite well and didn't leave as much of a mark as metal handcuffs tended to do.

When I turned, my eyes collided with the woman who'd been watching me. For just an instant, my domme mask slipped, my jaw dropping briefly before I snapped it shut.

Holy shit. Mariah Collins was here. I hadn't seen her since high school graduation seventeen years ago. Back then Mariah was the queen bee, ruling over the school with a signature brand of innovative cruelty that was likely unparalleled in the history of San Romayo Bay High School.

I had hated her. Hated. Her. Hated her with a passion that burned in my belly for years afterwards. I hadn't thought of her in a long time, but seeing her face brought it all rushing back.

Mariah had scoped me out as a target the first week of freshman year. I was impossibly awkward back then, with curly hair I couldn't control, thick glasses, second-hand clothes, and a face full of zits. I kind of looked like that little nerd girl in the movie who finds out she's really a princess and then her grandmother Julie Andrews needs an entire crew to fix her up.

Unfortunately, no one whisked me away to a tiny European country to show me how to straighten my hair or put in contacts. I'd learned all that in college. After earning a full-ride scholarship to an Ivy League college, I'd spent four years learning how to look put together, how to have high class manners, and most importantly, how to make money.

I'd made a lot of it. Growing up poor had sucked, but now I was in control of my own destiny. I was one of the most successful real estate tycoons in the state, buying apartments, office buildings, and high-end hotels.

Wherever I went, people wanted to be close to me. I had a lot of power in this city. People wanted to know where I invested my money. They wondered what neighborhood was about to become trendy. They wanted a donation from the foundation I'd created. They wanted to be photographed with me.

And here, in the privacy of Club Surrender, they wanted me to redden their asses and take their minds off their troubles. I was glad to be of service. After a childhood of feeling constantly out of control, now I craved control. Demanded it.

"Zelda Eldrich?" Mariah gave me a friendly smile. "Hi! I thought that was you. Wow, you look great."

Ignoring her, I returned to my submissive for the hour, giving her instructions for aftercare. She was lucid but floaty, and I insisted on taking her to the bar to get a bottle of water and a snack just to make sure she was okay.

Mariah inexplicably hung around, watching everything as she presumably waited for me to be finished. I continued to ignore her, although I couldn't resist checking her out from the corner of my eye.

She'd been super thin in high school, one of those girls who lived on diet shakes and lettuce and mocked anyone who ate real food. She'd filled out since then, lush curves softening her body where she was once mostly hard angles. She looked good at a more normal weight, I grudgingly admitted. Beautiful.

She was a few inches shorter than me, maybe five four or five five, her long blonde hair neatly styled and falling over her shoulders. Her make-up was light, wearing only shiny red lip gloss and a bit of eye liner that made her blue eyes seem larger than they probably were.

She was wearing a black leather miniskirt and a tank top, both of which clung to her curves. Long, smooth legs were encased in a pair of ankle high combat boots that gave her another inch in height.

If I didn't already know that she was evil personified, she'd totally be my type. Which just pissed me off.

"Mariah? Are you okay?"

Another woman approached us, her arm going around Mariah's shoulders. I wondered if they were together, then pushed the question right out of my head. I definitely did not care if Mariah was single, or if she dated women.

My stomach cramped as I remembered all the ways she'd tortured me throughout school. There was the time she dumped a red slushie over my head, ruining my brand new white shirt that I'd found at the thrift store with the tags on – a rare find. The way she and her minions had called me "Zit-face Zelda" for four years. And the time she threw the dodge ball at my head so hard I had to go to the free clinic and get stitches. She'd also broken my glasses, and because my mother couldn't afford new ones, I'd had to wear them taped together for months. Of course Mariah made fun of me for that too.

She had been a total bitch. A bully. And an all-around pain in my ass.

Suddenly I had an idea. She was here for newbie night. Maybe I should be a pain in *her* ass. I could show my bully exactly what it felt like to be tortured and abused.

No Zelda, I told myself sternly. *You absolutely can't scene with someone you want to hurt for real. You know the rules.*

I'd never abuse my role as a domme here at Club Surrender. No, whatever Mariah wanted to do here, it wasn't my business. There were plenty of dominants here who could fulfil her 50 Shades fantasy.

Finishing with my sub, I turned on my heel and, ignoring Mariah calling my name, I stalked out of the club.

Mariah

I watched Zelda march out of the club, back ramrod straight, the bright lights making the golden highlights in her hair practically glow. She hadn't said a word to me. Hadn't so much as acknowledged my existence even though I knew she heard me talking to her.

It was incredibly rude, but honestly, I deserved it.

I'd been a total shithead to her in high school. It was a combination of a bad home life, being totally freaked out that I was secretly bisexual, and the power of being popular going to my head in a big way.

After I drunkenly kissed my first girl freshman year of college – and as the song said, liked it – my best friend Amy had suggested that I go to therapy. I'd unpacked a lot of crap over those four years, to the extent that Amy and I liked to joke that it was a miracle that we were still friends, given that I was a completely different person now than I was when we met.

Coming face to face with Zelda was like taking a long, hard look at my past self. Two things were immediately evident to me. First, I needed to make amends to Zelda for all those years I'd treated her like shit. And second, I was in love with her.

With the maturity I had now, I was starting to realize that I'd had a crush on her back then. I'd been crueler to her than anyone else, but I'd also felt drawn to her, so maybe there was something below the surface there.

Maybe I was being fanciful, and maybe instalove only happened in movies, but I'd felt something when I saw Zelda tonight. Something big. And when I'd looked into her beautiful brown eyes, the past didn't matter. I wanted a future. I wanted Zelda.

I just needed to figure out how to make that happen.

"How's it going tonight?"

I looked up to see a beautiful older woman holding an iPad. She was tall and curvy and radiating self-confidence and power. Her silver hair seemed to imply that she was older, but her unlined face hinted at youth. There was something incredibly compelling about her. It was like staring into the sun, I was dazzled, but I couldn't look away either.

"Um. Fine, thank you."

"I'm Mistress Angela, the owner here at Club Surrender. Did you want to find someone to scene with tonight, or are you just watching?"

"Just watching," I answered. "But is there a way to request a domme if there's someone in particular you're interested in? Maybe for the next time I come in?"

Club Surrender had an exorbitantly high membership fee, but I'd gladly pay it to get a chance to see Zelda again.

"Ah, I thought I saw you checking out Mistress Zelda, she is one of our most popular dommes. She typically takes on one or two of the newer subs when she's here to play."

I didn't hesitate to respond.

"Yes. I want her. I want to be with Zelda."

"Let me see when she plans to come back. Give me your email and I'll see if we can make a match."

It might have been my imagination, but I could swear that I saw a twinkle in Mistress Angela's eyes, as if she knew my request was about more than wanting a spanking.

"Thank you."

A few days later I received an email from Angela at Club Surrender letting me know that Zelda had agreed to scene with me if I could come back on Friday night at seven. I was tempted to ask the club owner if Zelda knew my name, because I was pretty sure she wouldn't have agreed to play with me if she knew who made the request. Or maybe she thought this was a good way to get revenge.

Either way, I needed to apologize to her, and this was my chance.

I spent the entire week rehearsing my apology in my head. If it went okay, I'd ask Zelda to go out to dinner with me. And if that went okay, we could start dating. It might take a while, but hopefully eventually Zelda would stop seeing me as her bully and instead see me as her future.

Assuming she was single that is. I'd tried to stalk her on social media and came up empty. If Zelda was seeing someone or married or, God forbid, straight, I was going to be devastated.

On Friday night I headed over to Club Surrender dressed in a form-fitting red dress that brought out my tanned skin tone perfectly. I'd paired it with chunky black heels, pulling my blonde hair up into a high ponytail with curled tendrils framing my face. It wasn't really a BDSM outfit but then again, I wasn't

technically there for BDSM. I was there to apologize to the woman I'd mistreat-
ed.

Of course I wouldn't be sad if BDSM was also on the menu. I'd been dreaming all week about Zelda spanking me.

After I checked in a staff person led me down a long hallway with doors on
both sides. The woman explained that they were private playrooms. One section
had themed rooms, like a headmaster's office and a little girl's nursery. The other
section had 'all-purpose' rooms that could be adapted for various scenes.

"Mistress Zelda is waiting inside," the woman told me. "You all have this
room for one hour. Enjoy."

I knocked lightly on the door and stepped inside.

Zelda was in the corner, reading something on a piece of paper. She was
dressed in a form-fitting black dress and high-heeled black leather boots that
reached her knees. With her long, curly hair cascading over her shoulders, she
was a vision. Over the years she'd clearly learned a lot about looking her best. She
was stunning, no sign of the awkward girl she'd once been.

When Zelda didn't look up or acknowledge me, I cleared my throat.

"Strip," she ordered, still not looking at me. "Take off all your clothes and get
on your knees, hands on your thighs."

I shivered at her commanding tone and my nipples hardened against the fabric of my bra.

"I'd like to talk first please, Zelda, if that's okay."

Her head snapped up, eyes widening in surprise as she realized who I was.

"What the *hell* are you doing here?"

Zelda

When Angela told me that one of the newbies had requested a private scene with me, I hadn't thought too much about it. Newbies loved me because I had a reputation as a caring domme for first timers and they told their friends to request me.

I liked being matched up ahead of time because then I could come in and get started instead of talking to the people hanging out in the public areas of the club looking to find someone to scene with. With my career, I didn't have a lot of free time, so I liked to maximize any hours I could spend at Club Surrender.

"You didn't know I was coming?" Mariah asked, stepping farther into the room. "They didn't give you my name?"

She was wearing a cute little red dress and chunky heels and I wanted nothing more than to tear that dress off her and spank her ass until it matched the color of her dress. Then I'd kiss it and make it better.

Wait, what? Damn it. Ever since I'd seen her staring at me with those puppy dog eyes last weekend, I'd been having the most inconvenient fantasies about her. Sitting on her face. Fucking her with a dildo. Biting her inner thighs to mark her as mine.

The intake paperwork I'd been reviewing just had Mariah's initials, which we usually did to protect people's anonymity. I suddenly wished that the club wasn't so careful with people's identities.

"No, they didn't. I would never have agreed to scene with you if I'd known it was you," I said harshly, annoyed by my conflicting feelings towards her.

"Why not?" Her voice was soft and sweet, so different than that haughty judgmental tone she'd always used in high school. "I would have thought you'd jump at the chance to cause me some pain."

She wasn't wrong.

"Because as a domme, I need to be in control of my emotions at all times. I won't be able to do that with you. Not after how shitty you always were to me in high school."

"That's what I wanted to talk to you about actually." She gestured to the fake leather couch in one corner. "Can we sit down?"

I sighed as I debated her request. One the one hand, I wanted to tell her to fuck off and get out of here. On the other hand, I was curious what she would say. Curiosity won out. I moved to the couch and sat down.

"If we're going to talk, you need to be in a submissive posture," I ordered, just to see what she would do.

To my surprise, she dropped to the floor in front of me, resting her ass on her heels like a good little submissive. From my vantage point I could see down the neckline of her dress.

"You've gained weight since high school," I noted before mentally chastising myself for my rudeness.

Not that she didn't deserve it after the way she taunted everyone in high school that was larger than a size two, but I wasn't normally a cruel person. To my surprise, she smiled.

"Yeah, I'm in recovery from my anorexia now and able to maintain a more healthy weight."

She sounded proud, and I felt the tiniest bit bad that I'd always been so judgmental about her thin figure back in high school. I'd had no idea she had an eating disorder. Of course, back then I didn't even know what eating disorders were. Every girl in high school seemed to be on a diet.

"What exactly did you want to talk to me about?" I asked, suddenly curious.

"I wanted to apologize to you, Zelda. I'm so so sorry I was such an asshole to you in high school. I know I made your life a living hell and while there's nothing I can do to erase what happened, I want you to know that I regret it. Deeply. I was wrong."

"Why were you so horrible?" I asked, unable to stop my curiosity. It was a question I'd asked myself a million times over the years. "I never did anything to you to deserve that."

She nodded, her face etched with regret.

"Things weren't good at home. School was my escape. There I was like royalty, no one yelling at me that I was too fat or, uh, hurting me if I made noise or didn't act perfectly. That plus the hormones and the adulation of being the most popular girl in school, well, it all went to my head."

She met my gaze, her doe eyes pleading with me to understand. I noticed the blue almost looked green in this light.

"It's not an excuse, just an explanation. I want you to know I understand that. And also..."

She paused.

"Yes?" I prompted.

The words came out in a rush, like one long sentence.

"I realize now that I had a crush on you, and I didn't know I was bisexual, I didn't even know that was an option, and every time I saw you, I had confusing feelings and it made me hate you for making me feel things that I thought were wrong."

"You did not have a crush on me," I corrected. "I was hideous back then."

She shrugged. "I felt how I felt. I just didn't know what to do with it."

I searched her face but saw no indication that she was being anything but truthful.

"Why did you come to the club last weekend?" I asked. "Did you know I'd be here?"

"No, it was just a coincidence. But when I saw you flogging that woman, I knew I had to talk to you. All my bad behavior came rushing back to me and I wanted to apologize. Needed to apologize. And also, after watching you here in the club, I wanted you to be my first."

My entire body stilled. Surely she wasn't saying...

"Your first what?"

"My first domme."

Mariah

I stared up at Zelda, silently begging her to believe me. It felt like a turning point for us somehow, and if she could look past what happened between us in high school – how shitty I'd treated her – maybe, just maybe, we could do something about the attraction shimmering between us.

I wasn't sure if Zelda felt it, but I certainly did. Surreptitiously I glanced down at her full breasts. Her nipples were hardened points pressing against the fabric. Somehow, I didn't think it was because the room was too cold.

"Fine, I'll do a scene with you. One scene."

Her tone was aggrieved, but her eyes looked conflicted. I wasn't sure if this meant that she'd accepted my apology, but it was definitely a start.

"Let's talk about a safe word."

"Red," I said quickly.

She took a deep breath and a mask fell over her face. When she spoke again, her voice was harder. Firmer.

"You will address me as Mistress whenever we scene, understood?"

"Yes, Mistress."

"I will check in with you along the way and you will tell me green if everything feels good, yellow if you want me to slow down or ease back, and at any time if you are ready to stop, you will use red to immediately end whatever is happening."

"Understood." I paused, then rushed to add, "Mistress."

Zelda slid back on the couch.

"Over my knees."

I pushed to my feet, my fingers on the hem of my dress. "Should I undress?"

"Push your skirt up to your waist. Leave your panties on."

I walked closer, doing as instructed, and she leaned forward, landing a sharp slap on the side of my bare thigh. My skin tingled from her touch.

"You will always respond when you are spoken to," she chided. "BDSM is all about communication."

"Yes, Mistress."

Standing to the side, I awkwardly lowered myself over Zelda's lap. I'd never been in this position before, and it felt a little awkward. She shifted me so that my hands could reach the floor to brace myself. Without preamble, she brought her hand down hard on my satin-covered ass.

Thwack!

I inhaled sharply and she brought her hand down on the other side.

Thwack!

Zelda began spanking me steadily, moving from one part of my ass to the other. Sometimes hitting me harder, sometimes barely tapping me. I closed my eyes and relaxed into the sensation. It stung, but not too badly, just enough to get my attention.

I must have zoned out because I was startled when I felt Zelda reach for the elastic waistband of my panties. She slid them down slowly, revealing the round globes of my ass, and letting stop just above my knees. The slight restraint of my legs heightened my excitement, but not as much as the sensation of Zelda's palm sliding over my now-bare skin.

This time when her palm collided with my ass, I felt more than just a sting of pain.

Thwack!

Thwack!

She resumed her steady spanking, the sound louder now as flesh met flesh. Maybe it was my imagination, but I could swear that she was spanking me harder now. I supposed the first part was just a warm-up.

"You must be punished for your past bad behavior." Zelda spoke for the first time during the spanking, her voice firm. "You've been a bad girl, being mean to your classmates all those years."

"Yes, Mistress."

As the spanking went on, the pain bloomed across my skin, making it throb. I wondered how red my ass was right now. Gradually the pain turned into something more. A kind of release of my tension maybe. And then, after a while, I started to feel excitement, actually enjoying the sensation of being spanked. It was both liberating and arousing.

I realized that I was lifting my ass slightly to meet Zelda's hand. Moisture bloomed in my core, and I wondered if Zelda could feel it on her bare thigh.

Thwack!

Thwack!

The spanking stopped suddenly, the silence in the room almost deafening. For a long moment, neither of us spoke or moved. Finally, Zelda broke the silence.

"Where are you right now? Green, yellow or red?"

"Green, Mistress."

"Stand up then."

I slid off her lap and she grabbed my wrist, pointing with her other hand to a wet patch on her thigh.

"You dripped on me," she announced unnecessarily. "Your cunt was weeping."

"I apologize, Mistress."

"You found this spanking exciting?" she asked. "Sexually?"

"Yes, Mistress."

She stared at me for a long moment, then glanced back down at her thigh.

"Clean me off. With your tongue."

"Yes, Mistress."

I didn't hesitate to fall to my knees and lick my essence off her thigh. She parted her legs slightly and maybe I was mistaken, but I could swear that I could smell the musk of her arousal. I wondered what she would do if I kept licking my way up her thigh until I reached her center.

Zelda

Damned if spanking Mariah hadn't totally turned me on. My panties were soaked after a nice long session turning her pale ass a lovely shade of red. I'd never felt so aroused after a spanking session before.

For me, being a domme was about releasing tension. Feeling in control after growing up in chaos. I spent my days running my successful real estate empire and while I loved the work, it was a lot of pressure. Spanking a sub and thinking up elaborate ways to bring them to the edge of pain and pleasure was a release valve for me.

I was good at it and, better yet, I enjoyed it immensely.

Many submissives became aroused during a BDSM session. I very rarely even acknowledged that part of people's response, instead keeping my focus on the power dynamics and helping them reach their goals, whether it was to quiet an anxious mind or reach the floaty goodness of subspace. A lot of dommes liked to make their subs lick their pussies or bring them pleasure with their fingers, a bit of quid pro quo for their punishment, but not me. I'd never been particularly into that. At least not until now.

It had taken all of my control to not grab Mariah's hair and shove her face between my thighs as she'd licked her cream off my skin. I couldn't help but wonder if her arousal was for me, or just a biological response to being draped over someone's knee for the first time.

"Take off all your clothes and lay on your back on that table," I instructed, pointing to a table along the wall retrofitted with flexible straps on both sides.

"Yes, Mistress."

Maria dropped the panties that were still caught on her knees, then slowly pulled her dress over her head, leaving her in a demicup bra. Her breasts were larger than they'd been in high school, easily filling what looked like a C cup. When she reached behind her to release the clasp, I got a glimpse of dark red nipples centered in large, lighter red areolas.

My mouth watered at the sight. I'd always been a breast woman. I was dying to get my mouth on those, but not here. Not now.

Mariah walked to the table, gracefully pulling herself onto the cushioned top and laying down. I followed, spreading her legs wide and securing them to the table. She gasped as she realized my intentions. On her intake sheet she'd written that bondage was one of her top fantasies, right after spanking, and I intended to give her a taste of it.

"Pull your hands over your head," I ordered.

"Yes, Mistress."

The movement made her breasts rise up like an offering and I stifled a groan. Once her arms were secured to the top of the table I went over to the wall of supply cabinets, rooting around until I found what I wanted to use for this next part of the scene.

I started with a blindfold, wrapping the silk fabric over her eyes just tight enough to block out the light.

"Your color?"

"Green, Mistress."

Then I lit a candle. While I waited for the wax to melt, I walked slowly around the table, examining every inch of her curvy body. She was stunning. I longed to torture more of her smooth white flesh and leave my mark. Once the wax was pooling in the candle jar, I carefully dripped a few drops onto her breast.

Mariah yelped in pain, pleasing the masochist in me.

"Color?" I asked, watching the white wax harden against her breast.

"Green, Mistress. Is that...is that wax?"

"It is."

I dropped little beads of wax around her areolas, the sensation making her pull tight against her restraints. I knew the hot wax on her sensitive skin would hurt, but I also knew as the wax hardened the pain would be replaced with pleasure.

After I'd dripped a wax circle around the outside of each nipple, I blew out the candle and grabbed the vibrator I'd selected from the cabinet.

"You are not allowed to come," I said, my voice stern. "No matter what. Do you understand me?"

Her voice was breathy, telling me that she was already close even though I hadn't even touched her pussy yet.

"Yes, Mistress."

She jumped again as the buzzing of the vibe filled the room. It was a Magic Wand, guaranteed to have her writhing in agony in seconds. I should know, I had one at home for my own pleasure.

I put just the corner of the bulbous wand head against one nipple, and Mariah gasped, alternating between arching her back and sinking it as far into the padding as possible to move away. She couldn't move very far due to the restraints.

Once I had one nipple engorged and no doubt throbbing, I moved to give the other one the same treatment. When I glanced up at Mariah's face, she was biting her lip. I wanted to do it for her.

Slowly I moved the vibrator down her body, over the sensitive skin of her abdomen, tracing along the swell of her lower belly, moving from hip to hip. I loved that she was lush and curvy now. It made her softer and more womanly than she'd been in our youth.

I slid the toy down over the patch of hair on her mound, then down one lip of her vagina, and up the other, before I finally slipped it inside her channel. She was breathing harshly now, her hips punching up and down, and when I touched her clit with the vibe, she let out a little shriek. I moved away.

"Color?"

"Green, Mistress, but please, I need to come."

I loved hearing her beg.

"No," I said harshly.

She puffed out a disappointed breath.

I returned the vibe to her clit, circling it roughly. Her body began to shudder, and I pulled back, moving to trace her inner thighs. When she stopped thrashing, I went right back to her clit. Over and over I brough her close to the edge without going over, periodically reminding her that she was not allowed to come.

When she was sobbing, tears leaking from beneath the blindfold as she begged me for release, I turned off the vibrator. She'd had enough edging for tonight.

"Our time is up."

She lifted her head and shrieked. "What?"

I gave her mound a sharp slap, causing her to gasp.

"I'm sorry, Mistress. I need to come so bad. Please. Please let me come!"

I felt a thrill at how desperate she was, yet she remained compliant like a good little sub. This might be her first time trying out the lifestyle, but she was a natural at submission.

"I'll make you a deal."

"Anything," she sobbed.

"If you're a good girl and don't touch your pussy all week, I'll scene with you next Friday and maybe then I'll let you come."

I'd already decided that I wanted to scene with her again. I craved it, wanting to know how far I could push her.

"I...are you saying that I can't get myself off, Mistress?" she clarified. "At all?"

"Not if you want to play with me again. It's totally up to you. Do you want another round?"

"Yes, Mistress."

"Very good," I said, untying her ankles. "I'll reserve us a room for next Friday at this same time. Now get dressed. Oh, and Mariah?"

"Yes, Mistress?"

"I'll know if you're naughty."

Mariah

I can't say what possessed me to agree to Zelda's order to not get myself off all week. I mean, I didn't do it a whole lot anyway, maybe a few times a month, but somehow knowing I wasn't supposed to masturbate made it so it was all I could think about.

When sitting in a meeting at work, walking my dog, even while cooking dinner all I could feel was my core throbbing. It was worse at night, laying in bed with my pussy grasping at air, my mind filled with thoughts of Zelda. I had to shove my hands under my hips to keep myself from bringing myself any release.

Midweek my phone buzzed with a text.

Unknown Number: *Are you being a good girl?*

Thinking it was some kind of prank, or maybe a wrong number, I ignored the message. An hour later another text came through.

Unknown Number: *The correct answer is, "Yes, Mistress".*

Me: *Zelda?*

Unknown Number: *Do you want to try that again?*

Me: *Mistress Zelda, is that you?*

Unknown Number: *Yes, now answer my question. Have you saved your orgasms for me?*

Me: *Yes, Mistress*

Zelda: *Good girl.*

Damned if those two words didn't make my pussy gush. I wasn't sure exactly what was going on with me and Zelda, but I liked it. I hoped her attention meant that she was feeling the same pull as I was. I knew instinctively that this was not how she engaged with all the people she scened with.

That night she'd walked out on me, I'd asked the bartender at the club, a woman named Kristina, to tell me what she knew about Zelda. Kristina had shared that Zelda was a popular domme at the club, but she never got involved with anyone there. She didn't do a lot of repeats either, generally playing with someone once or twice before moving on.

By the time Friday rolled around, I was a horny mess. I dressed carefully, pulling out a little plaid skirt and white blouse I'd worn for Halloween one year.

I paired it with knee socks and Mary Janes, then pulled my hair into two pigtails, giving me a dirty schoolgirl look.

I couldn't say what made me want to dress like that, but it felt right so I went with it. Judging by the flare in Zelda's eyes when I walked into the private play-room, she liked it too.

"Why are you wearing that outfit?" she asked curiously.

"I don't know, it seemed like a good option," I said demurely. "It fit my mood."

"I should beat your ass for dressing like that," she threatened.

"I'd hoped you would, Mistress."

She watched me carefully, as if she was worried that I was messing with her, then seeing no artifice in my expression, she pointed to a wooden desk set up on one side of the room for just this scenario. Seeing the desk last week was what had given me the idea.

"Lay over the desk for your punishment then," she ordered in what I now rec-ognized as her dominatrix voice.

"Yes, Mistress."

Since she hadn't told me to undress, I leaned over fully clothed, the move-ment making my skirt ride up high enough that I knew she could see the bottoms of my white panties. I heard a sharp inhale and suppressed a smile.

It was good to know that I could torture Zelda just a little bit, given the way she'd tortured me all week.

She came behind me, pulling my skirt up to my waist, then pulling my panties down my knees. Opening a drawer, she pulled out a thick wooden ruler. I couldn't decide if I was excited or scared.

Definitely excited. That spanking last week had been incredibly hot. I'd never been so turned on in my life.

I was less excited when she brought the ruler down on my bare skin.

Thwack!

I heard the whoosh of air and then red hot pain bloomed, making my breath catch in my throat. Zelda wasted no time doing it again.

Thwack!

A little cry escaped my mouth. Fuck, that hurt so much more than anything we'd done last week.

Thwack!

Thwack!

Two more smacks with the ruler and I was crying.

"Shame on you for dressing so provocatively," Zelda said sternly. "You were a bad girl."

Thwack!

Thwack!

She paused, her cold hand running across my aggrieved skin. I shivered.

"Relax into the pain and you'll be able to take more," she whispered.

I forced myself not to clench my butt cheeks in anticipation of the ruler, instead relaxing my muscles and breathing out with every smack until I started to zone out. At some point Zelda switched over to her hand, easing up on the spanking. My skin was throbbing, the skin feeling hot.

"Your ass is the most beautiful color of red," she said softly, almost as if she was talking to herself.

Suddenly she slid her finger into my channel, spreading my pussy lips apart as she explored my folds.

"You're so wet from your spanking."

"I've been wet all week," I admitted. Then deciding to take a chance I added, "It's all for you, Mistress."

Her fingers stilled.

"What are you saying, Mariah?"

I shifted so I could look over my shoulder at her.

"I'm saying I want you, Zelda. For more than just a scene."

Zelda

My breath caught in my throat at Mariah's words. I'd been obsessing about her all week. Wondering if she was touching herself, thinking of me, or if she was following my instructions like a good little sub. Every night I'd lay in bed thinking about how she'd look when she came. Would she be a screamer? Would she be one of those women who came with only a soft sigh? Would she squirt?

I'd resisted masturbating, despite being hot for her to the point of distraction, wanting to save myself for tonight. Part of me was convinced that I'd see her tonight and realize it was all a weird little fantasy I'd cooked up in my head. There was no way I'd be this attracted to her. No way she'd be attracted to me.

And then she'd walked in wearing that damn Catholic school girl outfit and I'd almost swallowed my tongue. I'd never even known that was a fantasy for me, but I was pretty sure that for the rest of my life I'd think of her every time I saw a plaid skirt.

I met her eyes, searching, and saw only the truth shining there. She wanted me as much as I wanted her. She wasn't wet because she was a pain slut, she was wet because of me.

"Sit up." My voice sounded harsh.

"Yes, Mistress."

Mariah rushed to comply, shifting to her back and then gasping as she sat up and put pressure on her sensitive skin. I cupped the back of her head with one hand, drawing her closer, and gave her one last searching look. Her pale cheeks were pink, and her eyes were wide, excitement clear as day on her face.

I crashed my lips down, pressing against hers while I pulled her to the edge of the desk and shoved my way between her legs. Mariah immediately wrapped her legs around my hips and gripped my shoulders with her tiny hands.

Just like I'd imagined last week, I bit on her lower lip, hard enough that she cried out as she opened for me. Without hesitation, I slid my tongue into her mouth, aggressively exploring her until we were both panting heavily.

I pulled back just an inch or two and met her eyes. They were darker when she was aroused like this.

"I don't fuck my subs," I said solemnly. "Ever. But I want to fuck you so bad it's all I can think about."

"Maybe I can be more than your sub," she said hesitantly, like she thought maybe I was going to make fun of her or something. Given our history, I couldn't blame her.

"I'm attracted to you, but it's more than that. I knew it the minute I saw you last week. I want to have sex with you, but I also want to get to know you. Date. Maybe I can be your girlfriend. I mean, if you're single. I realize I don't even know."

It was cute the way she babbled when she was flustered.

When I just stared at her in shock, her expression turned uncertain. "Am I misreading this situation, Zelda? I felt like, well, like there's something between us, something I want to explore. But if you're not into it, or you can't move past high school, I totally get it."

I leaned closer until our noses were almost touching. "You're not misreading anything. I feel it too."

I couldn't say who moved first, but we flew together, kissing, touching, sighing as if we couldn't get enough of each other.

Sliding my hand between us, I parted her lower lips with my fingers then speared one finger into her opening. She gasped against my mouth. I added a second finger and began pumping in and out, fucking her with my fingers while she rolled her hips against my hands. She was slick with arousal, and it didn't take long until she was spasming against me, throwing back her head and crying out with the force of her orgasm.

When I removed my fingers, they were dripping. I pressed them against her lips, and she dutifully sucked them clean.

"I want to make you feel good too," she whispered. "Please."

My panties damn near incinerated.

"Lay back," I ordered, pressing my hand against her sternum.

She eased back down on the desk, watching me carefully as I reached behind myself to remove my leather skirt. I slid it down, revealing a lacy thong that made her eyes widen. I removed that too, then hopped up on the desk, laying on top of her for a long kiss.

When we broke apart, I crawled over her until my pussy was hovering over her face.

"Are you ready?" I asked.

"Yes." Her eyes were fixed on my smooth pussy. I knew it was glistening with arousal.

Slowly I lowered my hips until I was in licking distance. She reached out with her tongue and gave me a long lick that made us both groan.

"Sit down," she whispered against my folds. "Give me all of you."

I didn't hesitate, lowering myself until I was practically smothering her with my pussy. She began licking me eagerly, her tongue darting in and out as she explored me. Digging my fingers into my bare thighs, I ground against her face, silently directing her to where I needed her the most.

Mariah gripped my hips with her fingers, her hold firmer than I would have expected, and lowered me down even more as she turned her attention to my clit. She tapped it repeatedly with the tip of her tongue, the sensation making me almost crazy.

One hand shifted around my hip and slid up underneath my shirt, gripping one of my nipples through my bra. She pinched and kneaded my breast while alternating between tapping and licking at my swollen clit.

Unable to hold myself up as my orgasm approached, I fell forward, bracing my hands on the desk on either side of her head and grinding roughly against her face until everything inside me exploded.

Mariah

A gentle knock on the door brought me out of my stupor. Zelda and I were wrapped together on the narrow surface of the desk, her breasts right in front of my face, her chin resting somewhere over my head.

I couldn't decide what had been better: Zelda bringing me to orgasm after more than a week of anticipation, or the feeling of her coming all over my face.

When I'd first come out in college, I'd gone through a slutty phase, sampling every willing woman on campus, both the 'out' lesbians and the girls who wanted to experiment. Needless to say, I'd tasted a lot of pussy and I'd been eaten out more times than I could remember.

Even though I'd been more discerning as I got older, I'd still had quite a few partners. And none of them, not one, had rocked my world like Zelda, the woman I'd bullied and harassed so badly I was shocked she was even in the same room with me.

I was grateful she was, though. This had been the best night of my life.

When we heard the knock on the door, Zelda roused herself.

"We have to give up the room," she said, regret clear on her face. "They'll need to clean and sanitize it for the next scene."

She levered off the desk, pulling her shirt back into place and looking around for her underwear and skirt.

I moved more slowly, searching for my own clothes while a pregnant silence filled the room. I glanced at her from beneath my lashes, desperate to know what she was thinking.

Had Zelda's world been rocked as much as mine had? Was she regretting the decision to break her rules and have sex with me? She'd seemed to enjoy it, but was it as good for her as it was for me?

I hated to be this woman, but I couldn't resist asking, "So, what happens next?"

As she studied me, I hoped she wasn't going to suggest I see her next week, or even worse tell me that she'd scratched her itch and was done with me. Acid churned in my stomach as I waited for her answer.

She seemed to make a decision, striding towards me until we were only inches apart. She lifted one hand to push back a strand of hair that had escaped my ponytail.

"You're a mess," she said, almost tenderly.

Her hand shifted to cup my cheek, her thumb stroking across my bottom lip.

"I'd like to get to know you better," she finally said. "Who you are now. How you got here. Are you game?"

I nodded.

"How about dinner tomorrow night?" I asked.

"Like a real date?" she asked.

When I nodded, she said, "It's been a while since I've been on a date. I mostly only go out for business dinners. Where should I meet you?"

"I know the perfect place."

The next night I waited for Zelda at my favorite Moroccan restaurant. I'd made reservations just to make sure we got a table, since the place was super busy on the weekends. It was one of those places with high backed booths, dim lighting, delicious food, and attentive but unobtrusive staff, the perfect place for a date or a romantic evening.

I'd been excited about our date all day, unable to focus on anything else. I got to the restaurant a few minutes early and sat on one side of the booth, sipping a glass of red wine, while I waited for Zelda to arrive.

And waited. And waited.

I checked my phone about every ten seconds, but there was no message from her. We'd texted this morning and she'd assured me that she knew where the restaurant was, so I knew she couldn't be having a problem finding the place. She'd seemed as excited as I was about getting together, but maybe I'd misread her.

"Do you want to go ahead and order dinner?" the waitress asked.

I glanced at the crowded lobby, filled with people waiting for a table, and then down at my phone. It was seven thirty, and Zelda was already thirty minutes late. I had a bad feeling about this.

"I just need a few more minutes please," I said. "My friend should be here soon."

"We can't hold this table forever if you're not going to order," she said firmly, but her eyes were soft with sympathy, no doubt figuring out that I'd been stood up.

I texted Zelda asking when she'd be there, but there was no response.

At seven forty-five I texted her again, then when eight o'clock rolled around I asked for the check, taking my time just in case Zelda came rushing in. But no matter how long I stared at the door, she never appeared.

The anger hit as I left the restaurant. I thought Zelda and I were past what had happened in high school but clearly, she wasn't done punishing me for how I'd treated her. Standing me up like that was the height of immaturity. I couldn't believe she would treat me this way, especially after the intimate time we'd had together last night.

After we'd left the playroom, she'd bought me a drink at the bar, periodically leaning over to press a kiss to my cheek. Kristina, the bartender who'd given me information about Zelda on my first night, had subtly given me a thumbs up when she saw the lovey doveyness of the two of us.

After our drink together, Zelda had walked me to my car and kissed me until I was breathless, before demanding that I text her to let her know when I got home so she'd know I was safe. We'd exchanged several flirty texts last night before we went to bed.

I'd floated through the day, excited that I was finally in love, and with someone who appeared to be as into me as I was into her. When it was time to get ready, I'd chosen my outfit carefully, putting on my sexiest underwear and most flattering dress before fixing my hair and putting on make-up, something I rarely did.

Both men and women had sent me appreciative glances as I'd walked through the restaurant, but it had been for nothing. A big joke. A way to get back at me for being such a bitch when we were kids. All I needed was for Zelda to dump a bucket of pig's blood on me or something and my night would be complete.

Pulling out my phone, I called for a ride share. Since I'd been expecting to have a few drinks and maybe spend the night at Zelda's, I hadn't brought my car. As I sat in the backseat of the SUV that picked me up, tears filled my eyes. I was such a fool.

Two hours later, there was still no word from my date, confirming that I'd been blown off. Before I could change my mind, I blocked Zelda's phone number and went to bed, determined to put the whole thing behind me. I'd tried to embrace being in love for the first time in my life and had only failed. It was time to forget about Zelda and move on.

I just hoped I could.

Zelda

"God damn it!"

I slammed my hand down on the bar, making the submissive sitting next to me jump.

"Sorry," I mumbled.

After searching in vain for another way to contact her, I'd been coming to Club Surrender every night for the last two weeks hoping that Mariah would show up, but it was looking like she didn't intend to come back. Obviously, she was trying to avoid me, which I could respect if it wasn't based on false information.

"What's up, Zelda? You seem sad or something."

I looked up to see Kristina, one of the bartenders here at Club Surrender, giving me a sympathetic smile. Without asking, she poured me a shot of tequila and slid it over with a shaker of salt and a wedge of lime. I knocked it back in one gulp, not bothering with the salt or lime.

"There's this woman," I started.

"Is this the one you were all mushy with at the bar a couple of weeks ago?" she asked. "What was her name? Marie?"

"Mariah," I answered. "Yeah."

"What happened? You two looked pretty smitten when I saw you together."

"Who was smitten?"

I looked up as Lauren slid onto the stool next to me. Like me, she'd been a domme at the club for many years. She and the bartender, Kristina, had gotten together a few months ago and seemed really happy together. They exchanged sweet smiles that made jealousy burn in my stomach.

"Zelda and this girl who came in for newbie night, Mariah."

"What happened?" Lauren asked with a sympathetic face.

It occurred to me that being with Kristina had softened her. We'd known each other a long time and she'd never once asked me a personal question. I told the couple about Mariah's reign of terror in high school, and how we'd reconnected when she came into the club.

"Are you still mad at her about being a bitch in high school?" Kristina asked.

"No. She told me a bit about what was going on with her back then, which gave me insight into her home life and some other struggles she was having. She apologized, and I can see she's a completely different person than she used to be. I've moved past it."

"I don't get it," Kristina frowned. "What's the problem then?"

"My day job is in real estate development," I started. "I own several properties, including some hotels."

Kristina's eyes widened, giving me an appraising look. This is why I hated to talk about my job in social settings where people didn't know who I was. People looked at you differently when they knew you were extremely wealthy, unless they were also well off.

"Mariah and I were supposed to meet for dinner the night after you saw us. It was going to be our first official date. But I got a call that there had been a problem at one of my hotels. A huge tree fell and collapsed on part of the roof, damaging multiple rooms and sending a few guests to the hospital."

"We saw that on the news," Lauren said. "It looked scary. Was everyone okay?"

"Yeah, fortunately the injuries were all minor. But when I heard about the accident I raced out of my house to go see what was happening for myself. When I saw what a mess everything was, I knew I had to cancel my night out with Mariah. Except for one problem. I'd left my phone at home."

"Oh no," Kristina said.

"I don't know her number by heart or anything, and I was totally distracted with the tree accident, dealing with the authorities and checking on everything, as you can imagine. By the time I got home and was able to access my phone it was after midnight. I texted Mariah anyway to explain what happened since I was sure she thought I'd stood her up, but I got no response."

"She was probably in bed?" Kristina suggested.

I shook my head. "I texted her again a couple of times in the morning and when I got no answer, I called her. That's when I realized that she'd blocked my number. I don't know where she lives or where she works, and if she's got social media accounts, they're private. I'm at a total dead-end trying to find her."

"I have this friend," Lauren started.

"No!" Kristina said sharply. "You know that's technically against the law."

I smirked at the sassy submissive dressing down the domme.

"What are you talking about?" I asked.

"When Lauren and I first got together she asked a hacker friend of hers to find out my address so she could come to my house and beg me to give her another chance."

"I didn't beg you," Lauren protested.

Kristina rolled her eyes, then looked around to make sure no one else was listening.

"You don't need a hacker, I can help you if you promise to not tell my boss. Angela is a stickler for privacy."

I felt hope for the first time in two weeks.

"You can help me?"

"Yeah. I know where she works."

Mariah

I rubbed my back as I walked out the door of the Memory Care Home where I worked as a nurse. It had been a long day at work, with several of our patients acting particularly belligerent, and I was completely exhausted. It didn't help that I'd been sleeping like shit ever since Zelda had ghosted me for our date.

Even after two weeks my heart pinched a little every time I thought of her.

I got it, honestly I did. If I was her, I guess I would want to get revenge on me too. It's just that I thought we'd moved past that childhood drama. Our night together, that hot interlude on the desk, having a drink, making out in the parking lot, it had all led me to believe that we were on the same page. But clearly we weren't.

"Mariah."

I glanced up to see Zelda walking towards me. She looked different. Every time I'd seen her at the club, she'd been dressed super sexy in skintight clothes and sky-high heels, with her long curly hair falling around her shoulders. Today she was wearing a conservative pencil skirt that fell to her knees, a white silk blouse, and kitten heels. Her hair was smoothed back into a bun, and she was carrying an expensive looking bag. The change in her appearance was startling.

"What are you doing here, Zelda? How did you know where I work?"

I headed towards the employee parking lot at a fast pace, Zelda falling into step beside me. Her heels clacked on the sidewalk.

"Kristina at the club remembered you telling her where you work when I told her that I'd been trying to track you down."

"That's an invasion of my privacy," I snapped, even as I tried to figure out what it meant that Zelda had gone through the trouble of finding me.

"You blocked my number, I don't know where you live, and you didn't show up at Club Surrender. I didn't know how else to find you."

She grabbed my arm, her touch burning through the thin fabric of the scrubs that I wore for work.

"Please, Mariah, can we just talk for a minute? I have something important to tell you, and if you're still mad at me afterwards, I promise to go away and never bother you again."

I sighed deeply and pointed at one of the benches set up in the grass. When the patients were having good days, the staff or their family would take them out there to get some fresh air. Right now, they were totally empty.

Settling on the closest bench, I stared straight ahead, feeling Zelda's gaze burning into the side of my face.

"Well?" I asked impatiently when she didn't speak. "I've just gotten off a ten-hour shift, so if you could speed this along so I could go home and get some rest, I would appreciate it."

"I wanted you to know that I didn't blow you off that night," she began softly. "At least not on purpose. There was an accident at one of my properties and I had to go take care of things."

"Did the accident break your phone?" I asked.

"No. But I raced out of my house without it, and then I realized I didn't know your number. I had to spend hours dealing with the fire department, my staff, and our guests. I texted you when I finally got home, then tried to call you the next day, but you'd already blocked my number."

I turned on the bench, looking at her suspiciously even while hope bloomed in my chest.

"You weren't trying to get back at me for all the times I messed with you in high school?"

She shook her head. "I swear it. Google the Alton Hotel."

"The Alton Hotel? Wasn't that the hotel where a tree fell on the roof and hurt a bunch of people?"

She nodded. "Yeah, that's my property."

When I looked skeptical, she handed me her phone. "Google it, you'll see I'm not lying."

I googled the hotel and sure enough, I saw her picture on the main page. Zelda Eldrich, owner. She'd posted a statement expressing sympathy for everyone injured by the accident with the tree.

"You own a hotel?" I asked incredulously.

"Well, I own a few as part of my real estate portfolio. I buy commercial properties, make them profitable, then sell them for much more than I paid for them. It's what I do for a living."

"Oh."

That was so far outside my scope of experience I didn't know how to respond. I lived simply, and none of my friends were wealthy enough to own a hotel, let alone several of them.

Zelda grabbed my hand, pulling it into her lap, and my skin tingled where we touched. I turned to face her. Her gaze was open and sincere.

"Remember when we were at the club and you said you wanted to be my girlfriend?" she asked.

I nodded. "Yeah."

"I don't want you to be my girlfriend."

"Oh."

My stomach dropped. I tried to pull my hand away, but she held fast.

"I want you to be more than a girlfriend," she continued, and the squeezing sensation that had been in my chest since that night at the Moroccan restaurant eased for the first time.

"I want you to be my companion. My play partner at the club. And some day, my wife and the mother of our children."

My mouth dropped open. "What are you saying?"

"I'm saying that I love you, Mariah. If I'm being totally honest, I fell in love with you that first night I saw you at the club. The feelings have only grown stronger since then. Being with you was the best sex of my life."

"We haven't even gone on a date yet," I reminded her.

"Then let's go on a date. I want to know everything about you. I want to know why you became a nurse and how you decided to dedicate your life to people with Alzheimer's and how you take your coffee and what your favorite TV shows are."

"There's only one thing you need to know about me, Zelda," I said, sliding my hand up her arm, my skin sliding across the silk.

"What?"

"That I'm in love with you too."

She pulled me towards her, lips crashing together and tongues tangling for several long minutes before I remembered I was making out with someone right next to my job site. I pulled away regretfully, my fingers going to soothe my swollen lips.

"What happens now?" She looked a little vulnerable. I hadn't seen that expression since we were both freshmen in high school.

"How about we start with dinner?" I suggested.

Zelda's smile was radiant.

"Dinner's good."

She stood up and grabbed my hand, pulling me flush against her body. Everything inside me lit up with joy.

"But can we have dessert first?"

Epilogue – Mariah

One year later...

"Okay, this is one of your better purchases."

I looked over at Zelda who was reclining on a wooden chaise. We were on the balcony of a beach home she'd recently purchased from a foreclosure auction. When we came up here we'd expected to find a mess, but the home was in pristine condition, with a great view of the ocean.

Zelda was wearing an old-fashioned bikini that made her look a little like a pin-up girl. It was black with white polka dots, the bottoms high waisted and the top tying behind her neck with a large bow.

She lowered her oversized sunglasses, eyes caressing my curves. I was wearing a one piece with cut outs on the side that bared the skin along my waist and lower back. It was also low cut in the front, and my full breasts pushed against the edges of the neckline, a fact that didn't escape Zelda's attention.

"Yeah, I think I might just have to keep this one. It would be a good place for us to bring our family someday."

I sat up to face her more directly. "I want someday to be soon."

Zelda and I had been together for just over a year now. We'd moved in together nine months ago and were getting married next month. I'd wanted a small informal ceremony, but Zelda had her heart set on a fancy big event. We'd compromised on a formal wedding but with a smaller guest list.

"You're ready?" she asked. "We can start trying to have kids?"

We'd been talking about one of us getting inseminated. We were both the same age, but Zelda had lost an ovary due to endometriosis. She still had her uterus and the doctor had said it was safe for her to carry a child, but we'd decided that I would do it, at least this first time around.

I reached into the bag I'd brought out with me and handed her an envelope.

"I visited the sperm clinic. These are my top contenders."

She took the envelope, but her eyes remained fixed on my face.

"You're sure you're ready?"

I nodded. "Yeah, once the wedding is over, let's get me knocked up."

One thing that Zelda and I had realized once we got together was how similar our values were. Although we liked to visit the club once a week, we also ap-

41

preciated quiet nights and low-key activities like reading on the couch or watching a movie. We were like a boring old couple now, but we wanted more. We wanted to have a family.

She jumped onto my lounger, stretching out on top of me and burrowing her fingers in my hair.

"I can't wait to have a baby with you," she whispered, her lips an inch from mine.

"Me too."

"But first, let's break in this private deck," Zelda said, giving me a sinful smile. "I love outdoor sex."

"Sounds like a great plan."

***

You can find more of Reba's lesbian romances at
Books2read.com/rl/lesbianromance[1]
If you liked this book, please consider leaving a review or rating to let me know.

Be sure to join my newsletter for more great books. You'll receive a free book when you join my newsletter. Subscribers are the first to hear about all of my new releases and sales. Visit my mailing list sign-up at bit.ly/RebaBaleSapphic[2] to download your free book today.

Special Preview

The Divorcee's First Time
A Contemporary Lesbian Romance
By Reba Bale

"It's done," I said triumphantly. "My divorce is final."

My best friend Susan paused in the process of sliding into the restaurant booth, her sharply manicured eyebrows raising almost to her hairline. "Dickhead finally signed the papers?" she asked, her tone hopeful.

I nodded as Susan settled into the seat across from me. "The judge signed off on it today. Apparently his barely legal girlfriend is knocked up, and she wants to get a ring on her finger before the big event." I explained with a touch of irony in my voice. "The child bride finally got it done for me."

Susan smiled and nodded. "Well congratulations and good riddance. Let's order some wine."

We were most of the way through our second bottle when the conversation turned back to my ex. "I wonder if Dickhead and his Child Bride will last for the long haul," Susan mused.

I shook my head and blew a chunk of hair away from my mouth.

"I doubt it," I told her. "Someday she's gonna roll over and think, there's got to be something better out there than a self-absorbed man child who doesn't know a clitoris from a doorknob."

Susan laughed, sputtering her wine. I eyed her across the table. Although she was ten years older than me, we had been best friends for the last five years. We worked together at the accounting firm. She had been my trainer when I first came there, fresh out of school with my degree. We bonded over work, but soon realized that we were kindred spirits.

Susan was rapidly approaching forty but could easily pass for my age. Her hair was black and shiny, hinting at her Puerto Rican heritage, with blunt bangs and blond highlights that she paid a fortune for. Her face was clear and unlined, with large brown eyes and cheek bones that could cut glass. She was an avid runner and worked hard to maintain a slim physique since the women in her family ran towards the chunkier side.

I was almost her complete opposite. Blonde curls to her straight dark hair, blue eyes instead of brown, curvy where she was lean, introverted to her extrovert.

But somehow, we clicked. We were closer than sisters. Honestly, I don't know how I would have gotten through the last year without her. She had been the first one I called when my marriage fell apart, and she had supported me throughout the whole process.

It had been a big shock when I came home early one day and found my husband getting a blow job in the middle of our living room. It had been even more shocking when I saw the fresh young face at the other end of that blow job.

"What the fuck are you doing?" I had screeched, startling them both out of their sex stupor. "You're getting blow jobs from children now?"

The girl had looked up from her knees with eyes glowing in righteous indignation. "I'm not a child, I'm nineteen," she had informed me proudly. "I'm glad you finally found out. I give him what you don't, and he loves me."

I looked into the familiar eyes of my husband and saw the panic and confusion there. I made it easy for him. "Get out," I told him firmly, my voice leaving no room for argument. "Take your teenage girlfriend and get the fuck out. We're getting a divorce. Expect to hear from my lawyer."

The condo was in my name. I had purchased it before we were married, and since I had never added his name to the deed, he had no rights to it. There was no question he would be the one leaving.

My husband just stared at me with his jaw hanging open like he couldn't believe it. "But Jennifer," he whined. "You don't understand. Let me explain."

"There's nothing to understand," I told him sadly. "This is a deal breaker for me, and you know that as well as I do. We are done."

The girl had taken his hand and smiled triumphantly. "Come on baby," she told him. "Zip up and let's get out of here. We can finally be together like we planned."

"Yeah baby," I had sneered. "I'll box up your stuff. It'll be in the hallway tomorrow. Pick it up by six o'clock or I'm trashing it all."

After they left my first call was to the locksmith, but my second call was to Susan.

That night was the last time I had seen my husband until we had met for the court-ordered pre-divorce mediation. He spent most of that session reiterating what he had told me in numerous voice mails, emails and sessions spent yelling on the other side of my front door. He loved me. He had made a terrible mistake. He wasn't going to sign the papers. We were meant to be together. Needless to say, mediation hadn't been very successful. Fortunately, I had been careful to keep our assets separate, as if I knew that someday I would be in this situation.

Through it all, Susan had been my rock. In the end I don't think I was even that sad about the divorce, I was really angrier with myself for staying in a relationship that wasn't fulfilling with a man I didn't love anymore.

"You need to get some quality sex." Susan drew my attention back to the present. "Bang him out of your system."

"I don't know," I answered slowly. "I think I need a hiatus."

"A hiatus from what?" Susan asked with a frown. "You haven't had sex in what, eighteen months?"

I nodded. "Yeah, but I just can't take a disappointing fumble right now. I would rather have nothing than another three-pump chump."

I shook my head and continued, "I'm going to stick with my battery-operated boyfriend, he never disappoints me."

Susan smiled. "That's because you know your way around your own vajayjay."

She motioned to the waiter to bring us a third bottle of wine.

"That's why I like to date women," she continued. "We already know our way around the equipment."

I nodded thoughtfully. "You make a good point."

Susan leaned forward. "We've never talked about this," she said earnestly. "Have you ever been with a woman?"

For more of the story, check out "The Divorcee's First Time" by Reba Bale, available for immediate download[1] today.

***

Want a free book? Join my newsletter and a special gift. I'll contact you a few times a month with story updates, new releases, and special sales. Visit bit.ly/RebaBaleSapphic[2] for more information.

---

1.   https://books2read.com/u/bpznKX

Other Books by Reba Bale

Check out my other books, available on most major online retailers now. Go to my webpage[1] at bit.ly/AuthorRebaBale to learn more.

Friends to Lovers Lesbian Romance Series
The Divorcee's First Time
My BFF's Sister
My Rockstar Assistant
My College Crush
My Fake Girlfriend
My Secret Crush
My Holiday Love
My Valentine's Gift
My Spring Fling
My Forbidden Love
Coming Out in Ten Dates
Worth Waiting For
My Office Wife

The Surrender Club Lesbian Romance Series
Jaded

Hated

Fated

Menage Romances
Pie Promises
Tornado Warning
Summer in Paradise
Life of the Mardi
Bases Loaded
Two for One Deal

The Strangers Romance Series

---

1. https://books2read.com/ap/nB2qJv/Reba-Bale

Sinful Desires

Taken by Surprise

Just One Night

Hotwife Erotic Romances

Hotwife in the Woods

Hotwife on the Beach

Hotwife Under the Tree

A Hotwife's Retreat

Hot Wife Happy Life

Want a free book? Just join my newsletter at bit.ly/RebaBaleSapphic[2]. *You'll be the first to hear about new releases, special sales, and free offers.*

About the Author

Reba Bale writes erotic romance, lesbian romance, menage romance, & the spicy stories you want to read on a cold winter's night. When Reba is not writing she is reading the same naughty stories she likes to write.

You can also follow Reba on Medium[3] for free stories, bonus epilogues and more. You can also hear all about new releases and special sales by joining Reba's newsletter mailing list.[4]

---

3.   https://medium.com/@authorrebabale

4.   https://bit.ly/rebabooks

Don't miss out!

Visit the website below and you can sign up to receive emails whenever Reba Bale publishes a new book. There's no charge and no obligation.

https://books2read.com/r/B-A-IDTM-DVQOC

BOOKS 2 READ

Connecting independent readers to independent writers.

Printed in Great Britain
by Amazon

58322680R00036